LOOK OUT FOR THE WHOLE SERIES!

THE CASE OF THE IMPOLITE SNARLY THING

Hodder
Children's
Books

A division of Hachette Children's Books

**Special thanks to Lucy Courtenay
and Artful Doodlers**

Copyright © 2008 Chorion Rights Limited, a Chorion company

First published in Great Britain in 2008 by Hodder Children's Books

3

A Catalogue record for this book is available from the British Library

ISBN 978 0 340 95978 7

Typeset in Weiss by Avon DataSet Ltd,
Bidford on Avon, Warwickshire

Printed in Great Britain by
Clays Ltd, St Ives plc

The paper and board used in this paperback by Hodder Children's
Books are natural recyclable products made from wood grown in
sustainable forests. The manufacturing processes conform to the
environmental regulations of the country of origin.

Hodder Children's Books
a division of Hachette Children's Books
338 Euston Road, London NW1 3BH
An Hachette Livre UK Company
www.hachettelivre.co.uk

Chapter One

The evening wind howled down the badly lit main street of the village of Darkhyde. It whistled through the boarded-up shops and businesses. It twirled around the broken chimneys, and past a sign which read: "WELCOME TO DARKHYDE, Population 600." Someone had crossed out '600' and replaced it with '312', then replaced it again with '212'. Even more ominously, the '212' had a question mark beside it.

The wind snapped at a couple of letterboxes and scattered a pile of leaves across the street. Finally, it whooshed past a grocer who was closing up for the night, and disappeared back to the moor that surrounded Darkhyde.

Glancing left and right, the grocer shivered, shuttered his windows and began wheeling a cart of fruit inside.

"SKREEAWWWGHHH!"

The grocer whirled round in terror. Apples, bananas and oranges spilled to the ground as he up-ended his cart by mistake.

"Look out, everyone!" the grocer shouted. The fruit bounced around his feet. "It's back!"

He rushed for his shop door in a panic, but trod on a banana and went flying. Struggling to his knees, he crawled underneath his overturned cart.

Up the street, two portly gentlemen ran for the same doorway and got wedged in the doorframe. A passer-by struggled to enter a locked building, before skidding to a halt outside a shop whose entrance was marked by an ornamental jockey statue holding a lantern. In desperation, he seized the lantern and struck a statue pose beside the jockey.

Within moments, the main street was still and deserted. Darkhyde's newest statue tried hard not to blink as a large, hairy creature prowled past, waving its tail menacingly, before vanishing into the dark, following the wind back to the moor.

In the cosy study at Jo's house, the Five were poring over a large map which had been spread over the desk.

"Darkhyde is two hours by train," said Jo, pushing her dark brown hair behind her ears. "Or – though I don't know why you'd want to do this – eighteen hours by pogo stick."

"We'll ride our bikes out to the moors and find a spot to camp," said Jo's cousin Max. His blond fringe hung down almost to his eyes. "It's about a thirty-minute ride. Or twice as long by unicycle."

A thin, dark-haired boy in glasses pranced into the study in a pair of extremely tight cycling shorts.

"What do you think?" said Dylan, giving his cousins a twirl.

"I think you need more sun," Allie advised with a toss of her silky blond hair. "Your legs look like two sticks of chalk."

"I mean my shorts," Dylan said earnestly. "When I ride for a long time, I get a little bruised in the area of my bumpus." He patted his bottom in explanation. "So I need a cushion. By employing the latest life-raft technology, behold – Inflate-o-Pants!"

He pulled a drawstring at the back of the shorts, which rapidly inflated. A lot. So much that they up-ended Dylan completely. He ended up lying helpless on the floor like a turtle on its back, kicking his legs in the air.

"I think you've got more 'Inflate-o' than you need," Jo grinned, leaning down with her pen and stabbing Dylan's shorts with the nib.

PFFFTT!

The cycling shorts deflated, causing Dylan to rocket around the floor like a battery-operated hovercraft.

Timmy the dog pushed his brown and white muzzle up to the map as Jo, Max and Allie helped Dylan to his feet. He sniffed at the name "Darkhyde" and whined uneasily, as if he could somehow hear the disembodied, distant howl of a strange creature . . .

The next morning dawned bright and cold. Four day-packs were lined up on Jo's porch – black, grey, blue and pink. The pink one was decorated with concentric circles.

THWACK!!

An arrow thumped smack into the circle on the pink pack. Several metres away, Dylan stopped tinkering with his bike and looked round in admiration.

"Wow – brilliant shot, Allie," he said. "Are you mad at your rucksack?"

"I wasn't aiming at it," Allie admitted a little sheepishly, lowering her bow. "I was aiming at the shed over there." She pointed in the opposite direction. "As we say in Malibu," she explained, fitting a new arrow to her bow, "I'm tryin' to get my Robin Hood on."

Dylan pulled the arrow from Allie's bag. Red gloop oozed out of the hole.

"I'm afraid your bag needs a doctor," said Dylan. He scooped a fingerful of gloop on to his finger and tasted it. "Nope," he beamed, "ummm . . . strawberry jam. It didn't die in vain."

Jo and Max came out of the house, clutching bags of groceries.

"Keep practising, Allie," Max teased over the top of his bag. "You can protect us from the Mogow-Ki if we run into it on the moors."

Allie's eyes widened. "If we run into the who-dee-what?"

Dylan finished licking his finger and stood up. "Mogow-Ki," he said. "People near the Darkhyde Moors say this creature has been around for centuries. Even longer than Prince Philip. It looks like a cross between a huge wolf and a giant lizard, with shaggy hair and a long, scaly tail." He dropped his voice dramatically. "They say it has razor-sharp claws and vicious fangs, and it comes out at night to hunt . . ."

Allie gulped.

Max took over the story. "Apparently, there was this one time when the Mogow-Ki came slinking down the village street," he said. "Dozens of villagers scrambled up this long flagpole to get away from it, until the flagpole bent down under their weight. When one villager fell off, the flagpole whipped upright again and flung the rest of them as far as the next village, where they landed in a stretch of freshly laid concrete."

Dylan smiled at Allie's transfixed expression. "And we're heading straight into its lair, as if we're in the scariest film you've ever seen." He dropped his voice again, this time sounding like a film-trailer announcer. "A non-stop scream-fest of high-octane terror, and the worst part is – WE'RE GOING WITHOUT POPCORN!"

Allie yelped and released the arrow in her bow. The arrow flew towards the vegetable garden, where it hit a stack of seed bags. The seed bags fell on to the handle of a trowel, which flipped a set of pruning shears through the air. The shears whirled towards a hanging swing and cut one of the ropes. Instantly, the swing plummeted towards a group of lawn gnomes, knocking off their heads and turning on a garden hose, which made the hose twist violently and spray water all over Dylan.

"Yelps!" said Allie as Dylan spluttered and fought off the hose with Max and Jo's help. "Well, even Robin Hood could get startled." She brightened at the prospect of adventure. "Let's go to Darkhyde!"

Chapter Two

In the cold afternoon sunlight, the village of Darkhyde looked a little more pleasant than it had the previous evening. Several shops were open. A general air of neglect hung over the place like a fog.

The Pennywhistle Inn stood on Darkhyde's one winding street. Four mountain bikes were parked against the inn wall, while inside, the four cousins and Timmy sat at a table in the dining room. The ceiling was low and beamed, and the walls around the room were lined with old photos of a young female gymnast leaping, spinning and vaulting.

"So," said Mrs Downey the innkeeper cheerfully as she served out bowls of stew to the Five. "What brings you kids to our little corner of the world?"

"A very smelly diesel train," said Allie. "And I had a backward-facing seat, which always makes me all . . ." She twisted her hands around her head, feigning dizziness. ". . . wooooooooooo!"

"We're going biking on the moors," Max explained. "All the hills and dips – Zoom! Fwee! Phwoo! It'll be fun."

"Aye, they're fun all right," growled a wild-eyed, grizzled-looking local sitting at the bar. "You'll have plenty of fun." The cousins almost leaped out of their skins as he suddenly jumped to his feet, turned red in the face and roared: "UNTIL YOU MEET YOUR GRISLY AND HORRIBLE DOOM!"

There was a pause.

"Could you pass the brown sauce?" the grizzled old man added in a normal voice, sitting down again.

Allie meekly handed him the bottle of sauce from their table.

"Bicycling," said Mrs Downey, bustling back to the bar. "That will be fine exercise." She patted her middle. "You can tell I don't exercise much," she said coyly, "not since my gymnastics days."

"Oh, Mrs Downey, you're not . . ." Allie floundered, trying to be polite. "I mean, you look . . ." Giving up, she changed the subject. "We're also going to camp on the moors."

"Ay, it's the dark of the moon!" growled the grizzly old man at the bar. "The Mogow-Ki'll be out tonight! With its slavering fangs and its UNHOLY SCREAMING!" He leaned towards to Max, who looked nervous. "Want my onions?" he said in a low voice. "They make me burp."

"We don't believe in the Mogow-Ki," said Allie. She glanced at the others. "Right?"

The others nodded slowly. Timmy tucked his nose under his paws.

"Well," said Mrs Downey, "people here believe."

There was another pause.

"I'm afraid I snore a bit," said Mrs Downey brightly, "but there's room here for you kids if you change your minds about the moors."

"The moors!" shouted the wild-eyed old man. "Stay away from the moors! BEWARE THE MOORS!" Then he got up and added conversationally, "Well, I'm off to the moors . . ."

Grabbing a metal detector propped against the bar, he strode out of the inn.

"You see that gentleman, Timmy?" Jo said. "He's what we call a 'loon'."

Timmy arched his eyebrows in agreement.

"Ohh, Digger Pete's harmless," Mrs Downey said, seizing a wet cloth and wiping down the bar. "He just thinks if he searches long enough, he'll find the Hartington Jewels."

"Jewels?" said Allie, sounding breathless. "There are jewels? You said jewels – where are the jewels?"

Mrs Downey paused, her hand mid-wipe. "If you ask me, nowhere around here," she said. "There was once a famous film star named Dora Hartington," she continued as the cousins listened. "Wherever she went, she always took her jewellery collection. But when they were in the Darkhyde area, Miss Hartington's maid disappeared with all the jewellery, and it was never found." Mrs Downey gave a high, tittering laugh. "Pete thinks if he looks long enough, he'll find the jewels buried somewhere on the moors."

"Isn't he afraid of the Mogow-Ki?" Allie gasped, before adding hastily: "Which we totally don't believe in, by the way. Right?"

"Wrong," said Dylan. "Same way the kids in *Screamsickle* thought they were going to a perfectly safe ice-cream shop . . ." His voice deepened into film-trailer mode. ". . . until they turned up on the menu, and an ice-cream *sun*dae became an ice-cream *dooms*day!"

Dylan launched into a mad cackle, which made his stew go down the wrong way. The others patted him on the back as he coughed and spluttered. And outside, the moor winds tickled

the windows of the Pennywhistle Inn with their
long, icy fingers.

Chapter Three

The moors rose high and wild above Darkhyde. The cousins whizzed along an empty moor road on their bikes, with Timmy running alongside.

Dylan put on a burst of speed and disappeared over a low rise, some way ahead of the others. Jo, Allie, Max and Timmy followed. Mounting the rise, they saw Dylan's bike lying on its side in the middle of the road, its wheel spinning. There was no sign of Dylan.

The screeching wind obligingly fell away. Everyone shivered in the silence. Where had Dylan gone?

"It's kind of weird Dylan left his cap lying here,

don't you think?" said Allie suddenly.

She bent down to pick up a cap lying on a pile of leaves, lichen and grass on the side of the road. As she did so, a hand thrust upwards out of the leaves and grabbed her.

"Eeeaaaghhhhh!" Allie screeched, stumbling backwards as Dylan scrambled out of the leaves, grinning.

"Thank you, ladies and gentleman," Dylan smirked, bowing to the others. "The always-popular 'Hand from the grave grabs unsuspecting girl' trick. Never fails."

Allie whacked Dylan with his cap. Jo and Max laughed at the expression on her face.

"Girl whacks joker with cap," Jo grinned. "That one's a crack-up, too."

Timmy whined and ran off the road. He dragged the wreck of a motorbike out of some nearby undergrowth and deposited it at Max's feet.

"Speaking of crack-ups," said Max, staring at the bike, "look how mangled that front end is. Maybe some government experiment went wrong – let's say "Project Mogow-Ki" – and the monster stalked out here to the moors . . ."

Dylan played along. "The same way undead zombies stalk out of graveyards, hungry for human flesh . . ." He staggered around with his arms outstretched as Max laughed.

"Why can't you do scenes from musicals?" Allie wailed. "Or mermaid movies?"

She jumped back on to her bike and whizzed down a slope to a little hillock in the road. Using it as a launchpad, she pulled her wheel up and sailed into the air. Dylan followed, jumping the hillock a little higher. Not to be outdone, Max sped towards it at full pelt, jumped it and did a somersault in midair. Jo came last with a double somersault, a perfect landing and a smug smile.

Max narrowed his eyes. If Jo wanted a showdown, she'd got one.

Racing Jo back to the top, Max leaped on to his bike and pedalled like mad down the hill again. Jo gave chase. Dylan, Allie and Timmy watched as Max and Jo launched their bikes in unison, turned three somersaults – fell off their bikes and plunged into a muddy ditch on the side of the road.

Dylan and Allie burst out laughing as Max and Jo spluttered back to the surface. They failed to notice

Timmy throw himself sideways just as Max and Jo's bikes joined them in the ditch, showering Dylan and Allie with almost as much mud as them.

The rest of the day passed in happy exercise, fresh air, friendly squabbling and fierce competitions. The only difficulty was when Timmy leaped into Jo's basket, causing her bike to tilt forward and zoom along on one wheel like a unicycle with Jo struggling for balance on the pedals.

At tea-time, the Five found a suitable place out of the wind for a picnic. They unpacked their rucksacks and spread the contents on the picnic rug. Apart from Allie's oozing strawberry jam, the food had survived the expedition. If anything, it tasted more delicious than the Five could have hoped. Max threw an apple in the air for Allie to use as an archery target, but Allie managed to fire the bow instead of the arrow and missed. Arrow-free, the apple bounced on the ground and rolled towards Timmy, who picked it up and brought it to Allie. Shrugging, Allie skewered it on an arrow and raised it in the air, to mock applause from the others.

It was getting late by the time the Five had packed up their picnic, and the sun was low in the sky. Full and happy, they rode on in search of the perfect spot to pitch camp.

Dylan saw the old tin mine first. It stood on a hillside above the road, its tall stone chimney pointing to the sky like an accusing finger. The cousins pedalled off the road and pushed up the hill, taxing their mountain-bike tyres to the limit.

"Perfect," Dylan panted, reaching the old mine first and staring around at the dilapidated old building. He put on his best documentary-narrator voice. "An ancient Druid temple, where the mysterious pagans conducted human sacrifice, watering the earth with the blood of their victims."

Jo laid her bike on the ground and studied an old iron plaque set into the mine's exterior wall. "Hewitt Tin Mining Company," she read. Glancing around at the ruin, she added: "If I were them, I'd sack their cleaner."

"Let's set up camp here," Max said enthusiastically. "I can practice my rock-climbing. One man, alone against the elements, surviving against all odds."

He grabbed hold of a protruding brick, then started climbing the tin-mine wall. He had only got a few feet when he shrieked: "Aaargh – spider!", let go and plummeted to the ground again.

The others set down their rucksacks and unstrapped bedrolls from their bikes.

"Seems like a good camping spot," said Allie, shaking out her bedroll on a soft patch of moss. "If the Mogow-Ki tries to get us, we can hide inside the mine house – right?"

Timmy unrolled a bedroll with his nose.

"Thanks for making my bed, Timmy," said Dylan, pleased.

He didn't look so pleased when Timmy promptly lay down on the bedroll and fell asleep, leaving Dylan hardly any room at all.

"If there is a Mogow-Ki, I'm not afraid of it," said Jo firmly. She started hunting around for wood to make a fire. "Nothing's going to keep us from camping out here."

The sky thundered loudly. There was a flash of lightning, and the rain started pouring down.

"Except maybe that," Jo admitted.

Chapter Four

They reached the Pennywhistle Inn in the dark, drenched and cold. The fires that had been lit throughout the inn were a welcome sight. Mrs Downey left them to drape their wet clothes by the fire and settle their sleeping bags in the cosy dining room, heading to her bedroom with a cheerful "goodnight".

The Five wriggled into their sleeping bags and Timmy sat as close to the dining-room fire as possible. As the others began to nod off, Allie started brushing her hair. A lot.

"Ninety-seven," Allie declared at last, brushing vigorously. "Ninety-eight, ninety-nine . . . five hundred. There!"

"I'm glad that's over," Jo yawned, turning over and trying to go to sleep.

Allie tossed her head, flinging all her hair to the other side, and started brushing again.

"One," she began. "Two, three, four . . ."

The sound of loud snoring filtered through from the door to Mrs Downey's room.

"Mrs Downey wasn't joking about her snoring," Max grumbled, snuggling down deeper into his sleeping bag. "She's a window-rattler." He pulled a pair of cotton-wool balls out of his ears. "Even earplugs don't drown it out. Come and lie down on my head, Timmy. I'll use you for earplugs."

Timmy obliged, getting up from his spot by the fire and lying on Max's head.

"Hy mnuh," said Max happily from underneath Timmy's fur. "Smhuh hass hehhem."

Jo got out of her sleeping bag and headed for a nearby cupboard. She opened it, to reveal a black-robed, hooded figure with a skull face and wielding an axe!

"Hi, Dylan," Jo said. "Hand me an extra blanket, would you?"

Dylan lowered his axe and did as Jo asked. Jo shut the door in his face and headed back to her sleeping bag. Then –

"SKREEEEEAAWWGGHH!"

Allie dropped her brush, startled. Out of the window, a scruffy-looking kid their own age raced by, looking terrified out of his wits.

"It's the Mogow-Ki!" yelled the boy. "It's after me!"

Jo, Allie and Timmy ran to the window, closely followed by Dylan. Max found that his sleeping bag was stuck. He struggled to his feet and hopped across to join the others at the window. He was just in time to see a hairy, wolf-like creature, three metres from nose to scaly tail, chasing the boy up the darkened street.

Without stopping to think, the Five raced out of the door, Max hopping for all he was worth.

The village was dark and slick with rain. Along the street, villagers were shutting windows and doors as fast as they could. There was no sign of the boy or the Mogow-Ki.

The Five nearly jumped out of their skins as the boy raced out of a dark alleyway just behind them.

The Mogow-Ki burst out of the alley in hot-breathed pursuit.

"It's right behind me!" the boy yelled hopelessly. "Save yourselves! Better still, save me!"

The Five followed as the boy broke away and leaped into a dustbin, pulling the lid down on himself. The Five kept running, until they reached an old mill house further up the street with a water-wheel attached to the side.

"Quick!" Jo panted, gesturing for Max to sit on the wheel.

Max hopped his bag to the water-wheel and sat on one of the wheel's paddles.

"Top floor, please," he said.

Dylan opened the sluice-gate. Water gushed out and drove the wheel round. The paddle carried Max up to the roof of the mill house, where he hopped off in safety.

The other kids and Timmy rode on the wheel up to the roof, where Allie found a weathervane. She used its sharp tip to slice open Max's sleeping bag and free him.

"Now I know how a banana feels," Max said, stepping out of the ruins of his bag.

Down on the street, the Mogow-Ki sniffed at the dustbin. Then it swung its scaly tail at the bin, knocking it over and sending it rolling up the street.

"This is not one of my luckier days," said a weak voice from inside the dustbin.

The Mogow-Ki seemed to lose interest in the boy. It loped to a fence, jumped on to it and then jumped up to the roof of a building.

"Quick," Jo said, "let's see where it goes!"

They followed the Mogow-Ki, leaping over chimney pots and jumping from roof to roof. Sensing pursuit, the Mogow-Ki put on a burst of speed. The Five gave chase, getting tangled up on the way in laundry that was hanging from rooftop clothes-lines.

"Bad news, love," said the grocer, peering through his window at the five sheeted figures sprinting across the rooftops of Darkhyde. "Now the town's got ghosts, as well."

The Mogow-Ki leaped from a roof to a stack of crates, then to the ground. Timmy followed, taking a flying leap into a wagon full of straw while the kids slid down a drainpipe. At ground level, they chased the Mogow-Ki to a thick clump of

undergrowth at the edge of town. But before they could reach it, the creature had disappeared into some bushes.

Slowly, the Five pulled off their sheets and gazed at each other in disappointment.

A clanking noise made them look round. The boy's dustbin rolled up, crashed into a tree and disgorged its rubbish-covered and rather dizzy-looking contents.

"Oh, hullo," said the boy, struggling to his feet and swaying. "My name's Lucky. Thanks for helping

me get away from the hideous monster." He swayed
a bit more, and clutched on to the tree for support.
"Are you all spinning in circles?" he asked.

"No . . ." Allie said.

"I guess it's me, then," Lucky said weakly, and fell
back into the dustbin with a thump.

Chapter Five

In the Pennywhistle Inn the following morning, the kids fell on the full cooked breakfasts that Mrs Downey provided. Even Timmy had one in his dog bowl. They were discussing the Mogow-Ki in between mouthfuls.

"Maybe it's some sort of weird mutation," Jo said, munching on a piece of toast. She checked a list off on her fingers. "I mean, there's been that ugly prehistoric fish they found. There's a two-headed goat. There's Dylan."

The front door banged open. Lucky, the boy from the previous night, came into the inn with several bags of groceries.

"Mrs Downey," Lucky called. "It's me, Lucky. I've brought your food shopping."

As Lucky said this, the bottoms of the bags tore through and groceries scattered all over the floor.

"Bit of bad luck, there!" Lucky said, bending down to collect the groceries. "I'll have to come back with a fresh bag . . ."

Somehow, Lucky managed to bump a sideboard as he was picking up a tin of beans. A china jug wobbled on the top shelf, fell and shattered on the inn's flagstone floor.

"Might need to replace your grandmother's wedding china, as well!" Lucky called.

"I'm not sure 'Lucky' is the best name for him," Dylan said to the others in a low voice. "More like 'I'm A Danger To Myself And Others'."

Lucky noticed the cousins at the table and beamed. "Oh, hullo again. Some night last night, eh?"

"I'll say," Max agreed, mopping up the egg on his plate with a chunk of fried bread. "I wish we knew where the Mogow-Ki disappeared to."

"I saw my friend Rodney this morning, and he said he saw it headed towards Wendril Hill," said Lucky earnestly. "Then I walked into a lamp-post."

"Can you show us where that is?" Jo asked.

Lucky beckoned them outside.

"It's right there," he said, pointing to a lamp-post on the pavement.

Jo rolled her eyes. "Not the lamp-post," she said patiently. "Wendril Hill."

Lucky's face cleared. "Oh. It's about a twenty-minute ride that way."

Jo spun round to grab her bike. Then she noticed an arrow sticking out of her rear tyre. Slowly, she pulled it out. The tyre noisily deflated.

"Oops," said Allie apologetically as Jo glared at her.

"Oh, Allie, now I'm going to need a new tyre," Jo sighed. "I'll wait for the shops to open, and catch up with you guys later."

"OK," said Allie after a nervous pause. "We'll try not to get eaten by a monster till you get there."

With the others gone and half an hour to kill before the shops opened, Jo followed Lucky on a tour of the village. More shops than ever were boarded up, with sheets of plywood nailed across the windows like tightly closed eyelids.

"The town was pretty poor to begin with," Lucky explained when Jo asked him about it. "With the Mogow-Ki showing up, more people are leaving." He pointed to a building where an old red and white pole was slowly turning in the wind. "That's where the barber-shop used to be." He pointed to another building with a broken blue lantern hanging over the door. "That's where the police station used to be." Then, sounding a little more cheerful, he pointed at a shop further down the road. "That's where the baker is."

A man in a white apron with an armful of bread scurried out of the shop. After loading the bread into the back of a nearby lorry, he nailed several sheets of plywood across his door, hung an 'Out Of Business' sign on one of them, hopped in the lorry and sped away.

"That's where the baker *used* to be," Lucky corrected, as the cloud of exhaust smoke cleared.

"The man who sells plywood is doing well," Jo said.

Lucky shrugged. "He moved to another town. We have to import it."

The baker's lorry had turned round and

was speeding towards them. As it drove past, it went through a puddle and splashed muddy water on Lucky.

"About the only thing I know won't leave is old Pete out there," Lucky said, wiping the mud off his face. He pointed to the far end of the street, which ended at the edge of the moors. Pete was prowling around with his metal detector.

"He's always at the west end of the moors," Lucky continued. "I wish he'd find those jewels. I wish we'd get some money in town again."

He stepped away from Jo with an odd look on his face. Examining the sole of his shoe, he noticed a nail sticking out of it.

"I wish I hadn't stepped on that nail," he added, hopping on one foot in pain.

Jo turned round at a strange clanking noise that was coming from the Pennywhistle Inn. Mrs Downy was coming out of the inn's cellar doors.

"Mrs Downey?" Jo said in surprise, heading over to the inn. Lucky followed, limping. "Are you building a robot down there?"

"I was just dealing with my old boiler," Mrs Downey explained. "It needs lots of tending to."

She yawned, covering her mouth with the back of her hand. "Well," she said sleepily, "nap time."

She shut the cellar door. The door somehow slammed on Lucky's good foot. As Lucky hopped around, changing feet every time his other injured foot protested too much, a flower pot on a window sill above him teetered, fell from its perch and broke over his head.

"Are you all right, Lucky?" Jo asked in concern.

"Yeah," Lucky said, woozily rubbing his head. "But I really need a new nickname."

Chapter Six

Up on the windswept moors, Max, Dylan and Allie were whizzing along on their bikes again. Timmy ran beside them, his pink tongue lolling out.

"On the lonely moors," said Dylan in a hollow voice, "four Kirrins dwindled to three. Who would be the next to meet a terrifying fate?"

"I'd say the one who's about to hit a rock," Max said.

Before Dylan knew it, his bike had struck a large rock in the middle of the road. He flew over the handlebars with a yell. Timmy watched as Dylan sailed through the air, and winced as Dylan hit the ground hard.

"Hey," Dylan said, rubbing his bruises. "Look at these tracks!"

Max, Allie and Timmy joined Dylan to examine a set of large claw-marks in the damp ground.

"They're the right size for the Mogow-Ki," said Allie in a quavery voice. "Which way, way upsets me."

They followed the tracks off the road a little way, until the tracks abruptly ended at a marshy bog. Max studied the tracks closely, then plunged out into the bog until he was knee deep in the murk.

"Do you see any more tracks?" Dylan asked from the side of the bog.

Max looked around. "No," he said. He considered a moment. "But I seem to be getting shorter."

Allie, Dylan and Timmy watched as Max started sinking into the bog.

"I'm stuck!" Max shouted, trying to move his legs. "This is like quicksand! And it smells like the inside of my old trainers."

Allie pulled off her rucksack and laid it quickly on the ground. Rummaging through the contents, she pulled a length of clothesline from a side pocket. She whirled it over her head and tried to throw it to Max, but the wind blew it straight back at her.

Timmy seized the clothesline in his mouth and plunged out to Max, who clung to Timmy as if he was a life-raft. Dylan and Allie took hold of the other end and started pulling. But Max was still sinking. He and Timmy were too heavy!

Dylan dug his heels into the ground and tried to pull harder. Allie yanked off her belt. Ignoring Dylan's look of surprise, she tied the end of the clothesline to a buckle hole. Then she up-ended her bike. Tugging off the chain, she hooked the buckle holes over the bike's sprockets.

Realising what Allie was trying to do, Dylan ran over to help Allie turn the pedals and reel in the clothesline, Max and Timmy.

"They're too heavy!" Dylan panted. "Quick, Max – go on a diet!"

An extra pair of hands appeared on the pedals. Dylan and Allie looked up in relief to see Jo.

"Might work if I help," Jo offered.

Jo's added pressure on the pedals did the

trick. Slowly, the clothesline began to wind around Allie's bike sprockets, dragging Max and Timmy to safety.

"Thanks," Max panted, getting to his feet and testing the ground beneath him gingerly. "Remind me not to jump into any more quicksand bogs without a tow-rope. Or a submarine." He brightened. "Ooh, that'd be cool – a submarine!"

"We were following these tracks," Allie explained as Jo rubbed Timmy dry. "Max got kind of carried away. And he kind of carried Timmy with him." Allie sniffed, wrinkling her nose. "And you're wrong Max," she added. "It smells more like a dead starfish."

Jo had seen the Mogow-Ki track. She bent down to pick up something that had been pressed into the soft ground beneath the print.

"Before you went for your little swim," she said, "did you notice this . . . ?"

She waved a weathered slip of paper at the others. Allie took it.

"'Hewitt Tin Mining Company. Store scrip'," Allie read. "What's a store scrip?"

"Well, all those old tin mines used to have their

own money that they paid their workers," Dylan explained. "It was worthless anywhere else. Heh-heh – sweet deal for the company."

Jo took the scrap of paper back. "But how did it get from an abandoned mine into the footprint of a Mogow-Ki?" she asked.

"I say we should go and find out," Max said, sounding intrigued.

Allie sounded less convinced. "All right," she said, waving her hand in front of her nose. "But Max has to stay downwind."

They found the old tin-mine easily, by following the route they had taken the previous day. This time, they entered the derelict building and looked about.

"They call this a workplace?" Dylan joked, his voice echoing around the broken-down stones. "Where's the coffee machine? Where're the computers for wasting time playing games?"

Timmy started digging at the earth floor. It wasn't long before he had cleared away enough earth to reveal an iron ring set into a heavy wooden trapdoor.

"Aren't you clever?" Jo said fondly as Timmy tugged at the ring. "Some dogs find bones, Timmy finds trapdoors."

Chapter Seven

They hoisted the heavy door open, revealing a ladder leading down into the dark. Without a moment's hesitation, the cousins descended the ladder. Dylan brought up the rear. When he had reached the beaten earth at the bottom, he looked back up at the trapdoor.

"OK, Timmy," he began, "come—"

"WOOF!" Timmy barked joyfully, leaping down and squashing Dylan flat.

The cellar was damp and dark. A row of large barrels lined one wall. The rest of the room contained a number of strange, rusting implements: mining tools, wheelbarrows, picks and the hollow casings of old lanterns.

"The Mogow-Ki's got to be around here somewhere," Dylan said, getting to his feet and glancing around the cellar. "I bet we can catch it. Then we could put it on display." His voice rose in excitement as he began to picture the Mogow-Ki on a raised platform in a specially constructed cage. "The Eighth Wonder of the World, the Mogow-Ki! People will pay a fortune to see it."

Allie happily imagined them all wearing evening clothes (and Timmy a red bow-tie), parading on-stage and gesturing at the Mogow-Ki as the crowds cheered them on.

"And at the first show," Jo said, puncturing Allie's happy dream, "the Mogow-Ki will escape from its chains and run amok . . ."

Timmy growled.

"But it won't escape if we use the secret alien technology the government is hiding from us," Max put in. He pressed a button on an imaginary handheld device and aimed it at the imaginary creature standing with them in the cellar.

"And then we could the tame the Mogow-Ki, and it could visit sick children to cheer them up,"

41

Allie said happily.

"Or," said Jo, wriggling out from behind one of the large barrels with something in her hands, "the whole thing could turn out to be a fake."

She held up a hairy bodysuit and a Mogow-Ki mask. "It's just a costume," she said.

Timmy sniffed the costume. Then he poked his head into the mask, so that for a moment the Mogow-Ki was dog-sized.

"SKREEEAAWGGH!"

Everyone jumped as Max held up a battered old, hand-cranked siren. "It's an old warning siren for mine cave-ins," Max said. "That's how they fake the Mogow-Ki's howl!"

"But who's faking it?" Allie asked.

BOOM!

Above them, the trapdoor slammed shut, throwing them into pitch darkness.

"I'm guessing it's whoever just trapped us down here," said Dylan's voice, somewhere to Allie's left.

Allie pouted, although no one else could see. "Well, that's just mean," she said crossly into the dark.

"I've got a torch in my rucksack," said Jo's voice behind Allie. "But I can't see my rucksack."

Allie felt around in her back pocket and produced her mobile phone. She pressed a button, and the screen began to glow.

"Cell phones," Allie said admiringly, as Jo rummaged around in her rucksack by the light of the small screen. "You can watch webisodes, you can order pizza anywhere, and they give you light when you're buried alive. It's humankind's greatest invention."

Jo found her torch and turned it on. Dylan quickly climbed the ladder and tested the door.

"Locked," he said over his shoulder. "Of course that's what you'd expect, since they wanted us trapped down here. Still, one has to check."

"So we're trapped down here forever," said Max in a doomed voice. "Jo, I have a confession to make. I ate those cakes you were saving for dessert."

"Wait," said Jo, ignoring Max. "Timmy's found a way out!"

She shone the torch at Timmy. Timmy was energetically digging at the wall, which was crumbling away under his paws.

Max scratched his head. "You might've done that before I spilled my guts on the whole cake-eating thing," he told Timmy grudgingly. He knelt down to examine the place where Timmy was digging. "It looks like there's a tunnel behind this wall," he said. "Must be part of the old mine."

The others grabbed hold of the old mining tools and used them to widen the hole

"But who would trap us down here?" Allie complained, digging furiously. "I'm a guest in this country." She paused and yelled up at the cellar roof: "Hey! If you're up there – I'm just visiting from Malibu!"

"The only person who wants us off the moors is that Digger Pete," said Jo. "He's probably afraid we'll find his precious jewels."

Moments later, the Five emerged from the cellar into an underground tunnel.

"Jo, let me see your torch a sec," said Dylan. He took the torch and shone it under his chin. "I am the Undead," he boomed in his spookiest voice, waggling the torch so that his face looked extra weird.

"You're the brain dead," Jo sighed, taking her torch back and shining it around.

Tunnels branched off in several different directions.

"If we just wander around these tunnels, we could get lost forever," Allie whispered, her eyes wide.

"And we can't dig upward," Max added. "We'd cause a cave-in on ourselves. This is just where alien technology would come in very handy."

"There's someone who could dig us out," Jo said thoughtfully, waving her torch around. "Lucky says Digger Pete is always at the west end of the moors."

"Why would he dig us out if he trapped us down here?" Dylan pointed out.

Jo smiled mysteriously. "He won't know he's digging us out." She paused. "But we have to know which way is west," she added.

Max took an arrow from Allie's quiver and broke the metal arrowhead off it. He removed the string from her bow and tied the arrowhead to one end of the string so that the arrow-tip pointed sideways. Then he removed Allie's scarf.

"Your scarf," Max checked. "It's silk?"

"Yes," said Allie in confusion, "and it cost three weeks' allowance. Be careful."

Max rubbed the arrowhead on the scarf. "Rubbing the arrowhead on silk will magnetize it," he explained. "Then it'll point north . . ."

He let the arrowhead dangle on the string. As they watched, the arrow-tip slowly swivelled round to point in one direction.

"Bet your mobile phone can't do that," Dylan told Allie, gazing at Max in admiration.

"No," Allie admitted. "But I can text-message happy-faces!"

"Believe me, she can," said Jo in a hollow voice.

"Endlessly. Load up that wheelbarrow with metal tools. We're going to need them . . ."

Chapter Eight

Out on the west end of the moors, the sun was setting. Pete was patiently searching the peaty ground with his metal detector, singing to himself to the tune of Blow The Man Down.

"I've searched all my life and I've looked all around," Pete sang, *"Whey-hey, no jewels have I found! I live on the moors and I ne'er hear a sound, whey-hey, no jewels have I found—"*

PING!!!

Pete stared in astonishment as his battered old metal detector began pinging loudly.

"I've found the jewels!" Pete gasped. He started to dig. "I knew I'd find 'em! I'm not sure what to buy first! A solid gold top hat! Mexico City!" He dropped his spade, cleared the dirt away with his hands and—

Allie's head poked up out of the dirt.

"AGGGH!" Pete shrieked, stumbling backwards and holding up his hands. "A GIRL-HEAD!"

"Hi!" said Allie's head. "How are you?"

"You're not a fortune in lost jewels!" said Pete, calming down.

Allie scrambled out of the hole. "No," she agreed, "but my dad always says I'm a gem."

She turned round and helped pull Jo out of the hole as Pete watched in astonishment.

"We knew all these old tools would set off your metal detector," Jo panted, wriggling up to the surface and brushing the dirt off her clothes.

"And we thought you'd dig us out of the tunnel you trapped us in," Dylan said, pulling himself up with Jo's help before bending down and grabbing Timmy by the tail.

"Woof," Timmy complained.

"Timmy speaks for me too," Max added, climbing out last of all.

The cousins stood around Pete, folding their arms and fixing him with enquiring expressions.

Pete gestured to holes all around him.

"I dig and I search," Pete said, scratching his head. "I don't trap."

"Someone did," Max said. "Someone who pretended to be the Mogow-Ki last night."

He wielded the mask from the Mogow-Ki costume.

"Pretended?!" Pete cried out in shock. "The Mogow-Ki's a fake?!"

Lucky approached over the hill, carrying a shopping bag.

"Here, Pete," he said, "I brought you some soup—"
THUMP!

Lucky fell into one of Digger Pete's holes. After a moment, he popped up, holding an empty plastic container.

"Well," he amended, "I brought you a soup container." Noticing the Mogow-Ki mask in Max's hand, he gasped: "Wagghh!"

"Lucky," Jo said kindly, "the Mogow-Ki's as fake as a three-quid gold watch. Someone trapped us in a tunnel because he was afraid we'd find out."

"And we're going to find out who," Max declared.

"I can't wait to tell the village that we're out of danger," said Lucky happily. He turned to hurry away and stepped on Pete's shovel, causing the handle to snap up and smack him hard in the face. "Ow," Lucky said, rubbing his nose. "Except from shovels. They're still very dangerous."

By the time the kids got back to the Pennywhistle Inn, it was late. There was no fire in the grate, and no sign of the landlady.

"Mrs Downey!" Max called. "We need to contact the authorities! And we're hungry," he added.

They listened hopefully. All they could hear were loud snores coming from behind Mrs Downey's bedroom door.

"All this woman does is sleep," Dylan said.

Jo moved through the dining room, heading for Mrs Downey's bedroom. She tried the door handle. The door swung open. Cautiously, the kids and Timmy entered the bedroom, approaching Mrs Downey under her bedclothes.

Allie gingerly poked the sleeping form. The covers, which had been pulled up over Mrs Downey's head, fell back – and revealed a football, which fell off the bed and bounced away into a corner.

"Agggh," Dylan shouted, clutching Jo. "Her head fell off! Her head fell off!" He stared, and cleared his throat. "My mistake. It's a football."

Jo pulled the covers away. The only thing in the bed was a pile of pillows and a tape recorder. Loud snoring noises were coming from the tape-recorder speakers.

"Looks like Mrs Downey likes to trick people," Max said pointedly. "Maybe she likes to dress up like a Mogow-Ki, too. *Skreeeaggh!*" he added, in a decent attempt to imitate the Mogow-Ki's cry. He held his throat. "That actually hurts."

Allie shivered. "Well, I wish she'd keep the thermostat turned up while she's terrifying people," she said, clutching herself around the arms. "I'm freezing."

Jo suddenly looked thoughtful. She glanced round the room before going to the bedroom door and glancing out into the living area. "There are no thermostats here," she said. "The inn is heated with fireplaces."

Dylan frowned. "That'll probably reduce the

value of the house, but what does it have to do with us?"

"Earlier today, Mrs Downey said the boiler in the cellar was making a noise that I heard," Jo explained. "She doesn't have a boiler!"

Max kicked the football up to his knee, playing keepie-uppie with it. "How about we dribble her head down there and take a look?" he suggested.

Chapter Nine

Once again, the grocer of Darkhyde was shutting up his shop. Up and down the street, other villagers were doing the same. All the while, they glanced over their shoulders, ready to flee from the Mogow-Ki.

When the last light had been extinguished, Mrs Downey stepped out of a dark alley, a grim look on her face.

Meanwhile, down in the Pennywhistle Inn's basement, the Five were making their way down an old wooden staircase. Jo held her torch up high as they checked around for secret hiding places. Mrs Downey was clearly keeping something a secret down here.

Timmy leaped down to the bottom step, accidentally kicking the side edge with his back paw. There was a click. The step swung silently open on a side hinge.

"Hey," Jo gasped, leaping down the last step. "Look what Timmy found!"

Everyone gathered around the secret step and peered inside. Allie pulled out a handful of old newspapers that had been tucked inside.

"These are from 1926," said Allie, showing the others. "They're all about that Dora Hartington and her missing jewels."

"Wow . . . !" said Max, staring at the newspaper. "You could get steak and chips for one pound back then. Plus dessert!"

Jo pulled out a large piece of paper which had been firmly wedged at the very back of the secret compartment. She studied it. "This is a map of the village," she said at last. "All of these gardens are crossed off!" She paused, thinking. "When Lucky showed me around today, I noticed a lot of gardens with holes dug in them. He tripped in three of them."

"So we think this is a map to where the

Hartington jewels are buried?" Dylan asked. "And Mrs Downey is digging them up?"

"And she doesn't want people seeing her, so she scares them inside by pretending to be the Mogow-Ki!" Allie concluded. She frowned. "And yet she seemed so jolly . . ."

Jo looked at the others. "So," she said slowly. "If Mrs Mogow-Ki's dug up all these jewels . . . where are they?"

"Didn't you say you heard clanking from down here?" Dylan said suddenly. He crossed to an old washing machine which stood underneath the stairs. "Maybe Mrs Downey 'launders her money'!" he finished triumphantly, flinging open the washing-machine door.

There was nothing there.

"Nope," said Dylan, after a disappointed silence. "It was a clever line, though."

"And look at this," Max said, still studying the newspaper. "You could get all your washing done for, like, two pence!" He grabbed a handful of laundry from an old washtub beside the washing machine. "All this for 2p!"

As Max yanked the laundry, the tub tilted over.

Fistfuls of glittering jewellery scattered everywhere.

"Of course," Max added as the others pounced on the treasure, "the priceless jewellery probably cost extra."

In a Darkhyde garden, Mrs Downey pushed up her sleeves and began to dig. She was so intent on what she was doing that she was startled by a voice emerging from the shadows behind her.

"Trapping people underground isn't the best way to attract tourists to the area," Allie said conversationally.

The Five stepped out of the darkness as Mrs Downey whirled round. They surrounded the landlady.

Mrs Downey's shoulders sagged. "I was going to tell someone where you were," she whined, "once I'd found the rest of the jewels and got away."

"You're not getting away," Jo pointed out. "You're forgetting – we know what you're up to."

Mrs Downey's shoulders straightened again. "And you're forgetting," she said with a nasty smile, "I was once a gymnast."

In an instant, Mrs Downey had hopped to the

top of the fence that surrounded the garden, then up to the top of a wall where she scampered along and disappeared over a tall hedge. She raced away to the thicket of bushes where the Mogow-Ki had disappeared the previous night.

The Five watched her flee. They smiled at each other.

"She's quite nimble for a portly lady," Dylan observed.

Hidden from view in the thicket of bushes, Mrs Downey brushed leaves away from a board on the ground which covered a hole. She moved the board and climbed down into the hole, which opened into a narrow tunnel. Hurrying along the tunnel, she reached a door at the far end and pushed it open.

Stepping into the basement of the Pennywhistle Inn, Mrs Downey ran to the washtub, tipped the jewels into a sack and dashed up the rickety steps to the cellar door. She hefted the sack over her shoulder and flung open the door.

Dylan was lying on the ground outside. He was white-faced and vacant-eyed, his chest covered in gore. And standing over him, Digger Pete held a red, pulpy mass in his hand.

"Thought you'd steal my jewels, eh, laddie?" he snarled down at Dylan. "Well, I'll steal yer heart, and EAT IT!"

Mrs Downey shrieked and slammed the door shut.

Dylan sat up and wiped the flour off his face. "Don't know if they use flour and tomatoes in horror films," he said conversationally, "but it certainly says 'dead'."

Chapter Ten

Mrs Downey tried the front door of the inn next. She hustled out, still clutching the jewels — and ran straight into Max, Jo, Allie and Timmy on the porch.

"Good evening," Max, Jo and Allie said together.

Behind them, ranged along the street, were Lucky and various other Darkhyde villagers.

"What's good about it?!" Lucky moaned. "The village is dying off."

"But now people don't have to move away any more," Jo pointed out.

Lucky brightened. "Ah, right. That's good, I s'pose."

"And now that the jewels have been found," Max added, "they'll belong to the whole town."

Allie nodded. "Everyone will get a share."

Lucky's face split into an enormous smile. "There's that, too," he said. "This is the best night ever!"

"I found the map in my basement!" Mrs Downey shrieked as Dylan and Pete joined the throng. She clutched the jewels to her chest. "I dug them up! I don't care if they were on other people's property! I'm keeping them!"

She leaped into a gymnast's tumble and flipped off the porch, scampering to an old truck parked nearby.

"She's getting away!" Lucky shouted. "The night just got bad again!"

There was a roar as the engine spluttered into life. The wheels screeched and sent up a cloud of stinky smoke. As the truck sped away, Allie fitted an arrow to her bow, and drew back the string.

TWANG!!

The arrow ricocheted off a fence, off a boulder, off a lamp-post, and buried itself in the radiator of the truck which came to a steaming, hissing halt.

"Wait!" Lucky stopped tearing his hair out and

smiled with relief. "It's good again."

In the truck, Mrs Downey sighed. She slowly handed the bag of jewels through the window to Digger Pete.

"Nice shot, Allie," said Dylan approvingly.

Allie shrugged. "I'm better when I don't really aim."

Wreathed in smiles, Digger Pete approached the Five with the bag of jewels.

"Seems like you guys deserve a reward," Lucky said.

"Don't mind if I do!" said Dylan immediately, reaching his hand into the bag.

"Dylan," said Jo.

Dylan's face fell. "Just one diamond tiara?"

Jo looked at him.

"How 'bout a gold wristwatch?" Dylan wheedled.

Jo looked a little harder. Dylan sighed.

"Can I keep the football?" he muttered.

"It's all yours!" Max said, kicking Dylan the ball.

Dylan dribbled it to Jo, who kicked it to Timmy, who woofed and nosed it to Allie. And before they knew it, the village of Darkhyde were playing their first game of street football.

Epilogue

Out on the windy moors the following day, Dylan focused his video camera on Jo and Allie, who both stood on the side of the road looking confused.

"We're rolling," Dylan declared, flipping a little switch on the camera. "Sticky Situation Number 29 – You're Lost."

Allie improved her 'confused face' and cleared her throat. "I was sure there was a mall around here somewhere," she said to Jo. "I must have taken a wrong turn."

"Don't worry," said Jo, striking a pose beside her. "We can find our direction with a shadow stick. We just need a long stick."

She walked over to Max, who was about to take a bite of a hot dog. Before he could get his teeth into it, Jo snatched it away and propped up the sausage so that it stood on its end.

"We stand it upright and make a mark where the shadow falls," Jo said to the camera. She did this, marking an 'X' in the ground. "Now we wait fifteen minutes," she said, stepping back.

"But I'm hungry now!" Max protested.

Everyone stood and watched the sausage. It

wasn't the most interesting fifteen minutes they had ever spent.

"The shadow's moved," said Jo eventually. "We make a mark there." She marked the new shadow with the letter 'Y'.

"Y is west of X," Jo explained.

Allie lost her confused face and smiled brilliantly. "So that's south," she said, pointing to the left. "That's where the mall is!"

"And Timmy's running north with Max's sausage," Jo observed, as Timmy crept up to the sausage, seized it and ran off.

"Hey!" Max shouted, pelting after Timmy as the others burst out laughing. "That's my lunch!"

Read the adventures of George and the
original Famous Five in

Enid Blyton™

THE
FAMOUS FIVE'S
SURVIVAL GUIDE

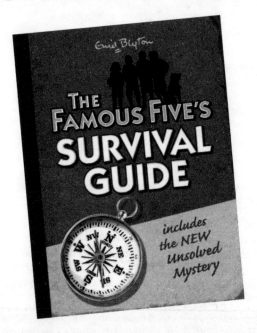

Packed with useful information on surviving outdoors and solving mysteries, here is the one mystery that the Famous Five never managed to solve. See if you can follow the trail to discover the location of the priceless Royal Dragon of Siam.

The perfect book for all fans of mystery, adventure and the Famous Five!

ISBN 9780340970836

driver was frantically radioing for help.

"This is the driver of the nine-forty from Langford," he shouted into his radio. "The electronic switches failed! We're on the wrong track – we're going to crash! Hello?"

Several miles further on, a second train was also on the track. And it was heading straight for the first.

"Maybe you can give me aiming lessons some time," Jo smirked as the boys wiped snow off themselves.

"No," said Dylan, shaking his head. "You seem to have it worked out."

Suddenly the lights snapped off. Everything went dark, save for the pale blue glimmer of the snow in the thin moonlight.

"Whoa," said Max. "Power failure – must be snow on the power lines. People will be stuck in lifts, if this town had any. Lifts, I mean, not people." He paused and brushed snow off his head. "Obviously there're people," he added. "I've seen 'em."

"How hard did that snow hit you on the head?" Dylan checked, staring at his cousin.

WHHHOOOO!

The sound of a train horn blasted through the air.

"Pretty hard," Max admitted to Dylan. "I hear a train horn over there—" He pointed west. "When I usually hear one at night—" He pointed east. "Over there."

A mile away from the cousins, a train was barrelling along the snowy, unlit track. In the cab, the train

"Because revenge is a dish best served cold," she explained, hefting her weapons thoughtfully in her hands.

"Well, serve it up," Allie said. "I'm running out of heat wraps."

Tugging a packaged therapeutic heat wrap from her pocket, Allie opened it up and pressed it to her face with a groan of relief. "Ahhhhh," she mumbled through the wrap. "Sweet, sweet warmth . . . Rats, it's cooling off."

As Allie opened another wrap, Jo finished making a crude catapult from the spade, the tyre tube and the timber. Timmy used his big black, brown and white paws to load snow on to the spade, and Jo quickly packed it into an enormous ball. Then she dragged the catapult into position.

"Hey, Jo," Max sniggered, "nice catapult! Too bad you don't know how to aim!"

Jo calmly aimed her giant snowball and fired. The snowball sailed harmlessly over the boys' heads, slammed into the steep roof of the house and dislodged all the snow which had gathered there. The snow promptly avalanched on top of Max and Dylan, burying them completely.

"You're wasting your time, girls!" Max shouted, pushing his floppy blond fringe out of his eyes. "You can't touch us in Castle Dylanmax."

"I don't want to touch you," Jo called, her dark face glowing with mischief. "I want to whap you with snowballs! Come out and fight fair!"

"Yeah!" said Allie. Trying to sound tough wasn't easy for a bubbly blond California girl, but Allie was doing her best. "And could you please hurry?" she added plaintively. "I'm very cold."

"Jo and Allie want us to fight fair," Dylan commented to Max. He took off his glasses and polished them before setting them on the end of his nose again. "Silly girls," he sighed. "Silly, silly girls."

Moving to the tennis-ball serving machine next to him – which happened to be loaded with snowballs – Dylan turned it on. The snowballs blitzed over the wall of the snow fort, peppering the girls and Timmy. They rushed to hide behind a tree near the garden shed.

"Remind me," Allie grumbled, wiping snow from her face. "This is fun, why?"

Jo grabbed a spade, a bicycle-tyre tube and some bits of timber that were standing beside the shed.

Chapter One

It was a quiet, frozen evening. Everything was still, all sounds muffled by the perfect blanket of snow which lay on the ground like icing sugar on a cake. Outdoor lights cast a warm glow on the whiteness, sending long navy-blue shadows where they caught the trees and shrubs.

"RAAARGHH!"

Allie, Jo and Timmy the dog hurled themselves over a hedge and threw snowballs at their cousins Max and Dylan, who were standing behind the sturdy snow fort they had built in Jo's garden. Max and Dylan ducked below the battlements of their snow castle.

THE CASE OF THE
PLOT TO PULL THE PLUG

Read on for
Chapter One of the
Famous 5's next
Case File . . .

Hodder
Children's
Books

A division of Hachette Children's Books

LOOK OUT FOR THE WHOLE SERIES!

THE CASE OF THE STICKS
AND THEIR TRICKS

**Hodder
Children's
Books**

A division of Hachette Children's Books

Special thanks to Lucy Courtenay and Artful Doodlers

Chapter One

In the cosy, well-lit study of Jo's house, the four Kirrin cousins studied the old map of Kirrin Island. The map had been hand-drawn into a brown leather journal, and was covered with promising scribbles like "Old Well", "Castle Ruins" and "Smuggler's Rocks".

"Wow, Jo, your mum and our parents had some wild adventures on Kirrin Island," said Max. As he peered more closely at the map through his shaggy blond fringe, he exclaimed, "I never noticed that big peat bog before!"

He pointed to a big dark splotch on the map.

"That's not a bog," said Jo. "It's a blob. A food

blob." She stared accusingly at her cousins. "Who's been sneaking toast and jam to Timmy?"

Hearing his name, the handsome dog at Jo's feet looked up with a "Who, me?" expression on his face. His muzzle was covered in crumbs.

Allie tucked a long blond curl behind her ear and sheepishly raised her hand. "I did it," she said.

Dylan adjusted his glasses guiltily. He and Max added their hands to Allie's.

"I think we need to cut down on treats," Jo said. "They're ruining Mum's journal, and turning Timmy into a tubbo."

Timmy lay down and hid his nose under his paws.

"Jo, your mom kept the most awesome journals ever," said Allie, flipping through the dark brown journal. "Listen: 'I was alone in the dark house; the only sound, the beating of my heart.'"

Dylan dimmed the lights for effect as Allie continued reading.

"'The hairs on the back of my neck told me that someone was watching, waiting for the right moment to—'"

CRASSSHHH!

An earsplitting noise made the cousins jump. Allie screamed as a weird shadow lunged towards the study window, and Timmy barked protectively. The Five surged outside to see what had happened. They stared in shock at the huge tree which had toppled into the house, damaging the wall and breaking one of the top-floor windows.

The dishevelled figure of Jo's mum George ran out to join the kids.

"Ah, is everyone OK?" she panted, looking around. "What happened? It sounded like a tree fell on the house."

"A tree did fall on the house," Max said, staring at the damage.

"Good call, Aunt George," said Dylan.

"Then Allie screamed like a girl," Jo added.

"I *am* a girl," said Allie in an indignant voice. "And I was all into your journal, about someone watching the house, waiting for just the right moment to . . ."

The others goggled at Allie in excitement.

"Well," said Allie after a pause, "I never found out what he was waiting to do, but I bet it was something creepy."

Deep in the shadows cast by the fallen tree, a mysterious figure pulled a phone from his pocket and flipped it open. He dialled a number and listened.

"The tree's down," he whispered into the phone. "We can start the operation tomorrow."

Chapter Two

The Five examined the tree by torchlight. Allie prowled around the edges, taking photos with her phone. There was a mass of branches from the fallen tree by the porch, and a pair of feet were sticking out from underneath

"Ravi, dear," said George, leaning close to the feet and sounding concerned. "Is there any damage?"

"It's OK!" said a strong Indian accent from somewhere in the foliage. "The herb garden is undamaged! There will be mint sauce for the lamb chops tonight! Mmm!"

George left her husband and approached Jo and

her cousins. "This was a healthy tree," she said, puzzled. "Trees don't fall because they trip over something."

"Look at the stump," Jo said. She pointed. "It's all mushy and yellow. Does that look normal to you?"

George studied the stump. "This wasn't routine root rot," she said at last.

"Routine root rot," Max said experimentally. "Routine root rot, routine root rot, routine root rot. That's quite a tongue-twister."

Dylan gasped in a dramatic kind of way. "Maybe the tree was . . . poisoned! Who stood to gain from its death? Did it know too much? Did it owe someone money?"

"We need to get to the root of this!" Allie announced, failing to notice what a terrible joke she had just made.

Max glanced up from the sandwich he was eating. Timmy was looking at him, making big eyes and whimpering appealingly. Unable to resist, Max tossed Timmy a piece of sandwich.

"Hey, hey!" Jo said, snatching the sandwich out of the air before Timmy could reach it. "We agreed

Two Ton Timmy doesn't need more treats."

Timmy worked his big-eyes routine. He waggled his eyebrows for extra effect.

Allie looked quite tearful. "It's just . . . he looks so hungry."

"Let's get him a steak!" Max cooed.

"Don't look into his eyes!" Jo ordered, shielding her face with her arms. "They have power! Look away! Sorry, boy," she continued from the safe confines of her hoodie sleeves. "From now on, it's diet and exercise for you."

Timmy made a disgusted noise in protest.

A branch overhead creaked and scattered fistfuls of leaves on to George's face. Amused, Allie snapped a photo.

"What a mess," George said, pulling leaves off her and peering into the tree. "We're going to need a professional to deal with all this damage."

A cheerful voice spoke up from the darkness.

"Well then, I'm your man!"

A smiling, chubby man with bad skin stepped up to the Kirrins, munching on crisps from a small bag. He was with a pretty girl who looked about fifteen

years old. Both were wearing overalls.

"Ed Gumptybum," said the man between mouthfuls of crisps. "Handyman *extraordinaire*. And my daughter *extraordinaire*, Gwen."

The pretty girl gave a shy wave.

"Oh," said Jo in recognition. "You were here a few weeks ago looking for plumbing jobs."

Ed Gumptybum waved his hand. "And before that, gardening. I'm a man of many trades. If you ever need a magician, call me." Reaching out, he pulled a coin from behind Dylan's ear. "Bet you didn't know you had 50 pence behind your ear," he told Dylan.

"Yes, I did," said Dylan. "Give it back." And he snatched the coin back.

"You look like a hard worker, Mr Gumptybum," said Ravi, still beneath the tree. "You've got the job."

Gwen smiled. "Bravo, Daddy!" she said. "I'll get your tools from the van."

"What a relief," said George as Gwen headed for Ed's van, which was parked a little distance away. "A skilled handyman-cum-tree remover. Perfect timing!"

Jo was staring at Ed Gumptybum with a

thoughtful expression on her face. "Yeah," she said. "I suppose so . . ."

Chapter Three

The following day, the cousins gathered in the study again. Dylan was at his laptop. Timmy was eyeing Dylan's sandwich, which sat on the desk beside him.

"Ah-ha!" said Dylan. "Metadexahydratin!"

Timmy inched a footstool towards the desk, then pushed a phonebook next to the footstool. He began to climb up the makeshift staircase towards the sandwich.

"Whosie-whatsa-whatsa-who?" Allie said in confusion, leaning over Dylan's shoulder to see the screen properly.

Timmy made a grab for the sandwich – but Jo

snatched it away just in time.

"Break time's over, Timmy," Jo said. She led Timmy to an electric treadmill in the corner of the study, and switched it on. "Give me another hundred laps, then you can have a rice cake. Half a rice cake," she amended.

With a sigh, Timmy climbed on to the treadmill and started trotting.

"Metadexahydratin is an acid for cleaning bricks and stone," Dylan read out from the screen, as the treadmill whirred in the background. "But if you put it on healthy wood, it turns it into a squishy mush that smells like rotten eggs."

"My mum does that to roast beef," Max said.

"This says metadexahydratin turns purple if you add vegetable glycerin," Dylan continued.

"My make-up remover is mostly vegetable glycerin," said Allie, digging through her purse and removing a small jar which she put on the desk. "Solves crimes *and* it moistens my skin."

Jo pulled out a plastic bag with a chunk of yellow, pulpy wood in it. She opened the bag, and Allie dripped some glycerin on it.

The wood fizzed and turned purple. The cousins

studied it for a moment. Then they wrinkled their noses.

"They said it turns purple," Max said, backing off. "They didn't say it smells like vulture vomit."

"So the tree *was* poisoned!" Allie concluded triumphantly. "By whosie-whatsa-whatsa-who!"

"But where do you get it?" Dylan wanted to know. "I don't recall seeing 'Whosie-whatsa-whatsa-who' on my supermarket shelf."

"There's a DIY shop in the village," Jo said suddenly. "It might be on their shelves."

She rushed out of the study, followed by Max and Allie. Dylan shut down his laptop and picked up his sandwich. He noticed Timmy looking at him with the Big Eyes.

"Cut it out," Dylan said, transfixed. "Don't look at me like that. Jo doesn't want – aw, I suppose one sandwich couldn't hurt."

He handed Timmy the sandwich. Timmy wolfed it down happily.

"Don't tell anybody," Dylan advised, as Timmy followed him out of the room.

Upstairs in George and Ravi's bedroom, Ed

12

Gumptybum, his daughter Gwen and George were studying the tree limbs poking in through the broken window. The branches and leaves filled half the room.

"I've always enjoyed houseplants," George said, "but this is simply excessive."

"Oh dear, oh dear," Ed Gumptybum murmured, studying the ceiling and munching his crisps. "Main support beam's more cracked than me Uncle Sid. And he thought he was a canal barge."

"Does that mean the roof could fall, Daddy?" said Gwen. She sounded odd, as if she was reading from a script.

"Just so, Sweetums," Ed said. "What I need is a steel support strut. But I'm afraid to leave this unattended." He waved his arms in the air. "CRASH!" he added meaningfully.

"Maybe Mr Ravi and Ms George could go to town and get one," Gwen continued, still sounding odd.

"By all means," George said. "I'll get Ravi and we'll leave straight away."

She left the bedroom, shaking her head.

Gwen's pretty-little-girl act dropped. Suddenly,

she sounded a whole lot tougher. "I didn't think the old bat would ever leave," she snarled.

"There's no time to lose," Ed said, dropping his crisp packet. Crumbs scattered all over the floor. "We've got to find that journal."

"Chill, Dad," Gwen drawled. "How hard can it be to find a stupid journal?"

Chapter Four

Ed Gumptybum and his daughter dashed downstairs. The house was deserted so they made straight for the study. Stacks of old journals were lying on the floor, books and papers strewn around every available surface.

"Oh, this is insane," Gwen said, grabbing journal after journal and tossing them back to the floor. "This woman must've done nothing but keep journals." She picked out a passage in the journal she was about to hurl away: "'And then we had ham sandwiches, biscuits and great lashings of ginger beer.' She and her cousins spent all their time eating!"

"Here we go!" Ed said eagerly, seizing a grubby little journal that was almost hidden beneath the papers on the desk. "Her entries on 'Old Spotty Face'. She even drew a picture . . ."

Reaching over, he showed Gwen the journal.

"Hoo!" Gwen winced, laughing. "He was an ugly little rodent, wasn't he?"

Ed shut the journal, a sour look on his face. "That's me," he snapped. "I was 'Old Spotty Face'."

"You were who?" said George, standing stock-still in the doorway with two scatter-cushions in her arms. She set the cushions down and snatched the journal from a startled Ed Gumptybum. "What are you doing with my journal?"

"Um . . ." said Ed, unable to think of an excuse. "What are you doing back so soon?"

"We had to empty our car if we're going to bring home a support strut," George growled, glaring at Ed. "And 'Old Spotty Face' was Edgar Stick, not Ed Gumptybum."

"Gumptybum's the name of the foster family that I went to live with after you and your rotten cousins got my mum and dad arrested," said Ed shrilly.

George pointed an accusing finger at the shifty-looking man. "Your mum and dad were thieves and smugglers," she said.

Unmoved, Ed shrugged. "Nobody's perfect," he said. "Like me – *I* can't remember how to find the dungeons on Kirrin Island. And there's still some valuable loot down there nobody ever found. So I need the map you drew in your journal." He beckoned for the journal in George's hand. "Hand it over, dear."

George took a fistful of paper and ripped a great section of pages out of the journal. She tore them in half and threw them around the room, adding to the paper chaos.

"That's all you'll ever get of my journal," George snarled.

"See," Ed Gumptybum said, moving quickly towards George, "now we have to do things the hard way. You'll have to show me the island in person."

He lunged at George to grab her. But George ducked away, and Ed landed in a large rolling desk-chair. George gave the chair a shove, and it crashed into a wall on the far side of the room. Before Ed

could react, George had grabbed a small heavy bust of Shakespeare off a nearby table and hurled it at the support holding up a shelf of books directly above the chair. With a crash, the shelf collapsed and dumped its contents on top of Ed Gumptybum.

As Gwen ran to help her father out from beneath the books, George quickly opened a desk drawer and pulled out a key on a yellow keychain. She wedged it into the frame of an oil painting on the wall, a painting of Kirrin Island.

"George dear," said Ravi, his view obscured by a tall stack of scatter-cushions in his arms as he stood in the doorway of the study, "why did we buy so many cushions? This really is a lot of cushions."

Gwen stuck out her foot and tripped Ravi up. Ravi went sprawling to the ground in a heap of cushions.

"Oof!" Ravi spluttered from the ground. "At least I landed on a cushion."

Gwen threw herself on top of him, pinning Ravi down.

"But now someone is sitting on my head," Ravi continued in a muffled voice, "which I find to be most unpleasant."

George started towards Ravi. But Ed Gumptybum tore a curtain from a window and threw it over George like a net.

"Gwen, darling," Ed said, pinioning George in the curtain and hustling her towards the door. "It looks like the Kirrin Island dungeons just got themselves some new prisoners."

The Five made their way through the gates of the builders' yard, having drawn a blank at the DIY

shop. The yard was an open lot, with pallets of stacked bricks and wire containers containing various kinds of stone. Glancing around, they headed across the yard.

"Five pounds of rocks cost ten pounds of money?" Dylan gasped, gawping at the prices that hung on the wire containers. "I've got to get into this racket."

Max pulled a piece of beef jerky from his pocket and started chewing it as the Five approached an open shed which appeared to serve as the office. A large, cheerful man stood behind the counter.

"Excuse me," said Jo, "do you work here?"

In the background, a worker carried a heavy boulder across the yard and heaved it into a wire container full of similar-sized boulders.

"I own the place," said the cheerful man, raising his voice over the noise of the boulder clattering into the container. "'Mr Brick' they call me. That's a business nickname," he added. "Real name's Stoney Granite."

Allie smiled. "Do you by any chance sell meta . . . meta . . ." She clicked her fingers. "Take it, Dylan."

"Metadexahydratin," Dylan supplied.

Stoney Granite shrugged. "Sold some last week."

There was a crash in the background as the workman tipped another boulder into the wire container. The container promptly gave way and scattered the boulders across the yard. Sighing, the worker began heaving the boulders back into a pile.

"This guy who bought the meta . . . etcetera," Allie continued. "Was he about forty, bad skin, pulled stuff out of your ears?"

"Wow!" said Stoney Granite, looking impressed. Then: "No, he was nothing like that. It was Freddy Tucker."

"Al Fresco Freddy?" Jo frowned. "The weird guy who lives in a cabbage field and collects old cans?"

"I hear he has a ball of aluminium foil the size of a London taxi!" said Max in an awed voice.

"Why would he poison a poor, innocent tree?" Allie asked.

Dylan made a big show of scratching his chin. "Well, let's see . . . Far-fetched though it may seem, I propose it's because HE'S A STARK RAVING LOONEY!"

"Well," said Jo, thumping the counter as she

made a decision. "We're going to pay a visit to the stark raving looney."

Chapter Five

Jo strode out of the office, followed by Dylan and Allie. Max stared down at Timmy, who was gazing at his beef jerky. He flinched as Timmy fixed him with the Big Eyes.

"Ohhh," Max said, flapping his hands, "there're those eyes . . ."

Timmy's eyes melted into even deeper pools of longing.

"All right," Max sighed, lobbing Timmy his jerky. "I guess one bit of beef jerky can't hurt."

"Max?" Jo said, putting her head back through the office door. "What are you waiting for?"

"Oh, er, I was just . . . buying a brick!" Max said

nervously as Timmy retreated to a safe corner with his treat. "You know, my dad's birthday's coming up . . ."

Flustered, Max picked up a brick, put some money on the counter and ran after Jo with Timmy close at his heels. Scratching his head as he took the coins, Mr Stoney Granite watched them go.

In a dingy alleyway a little while later, a bearded, wild-eyed old hippie-type was rummaging in dustbins behind a grocer's shop.

"Ah-ha!" he croaked, pouncing on a scrap of shining silver foil.

Very carefully, he added it to the enormous ball of foil that was leaning against the alleyway wall. The ball was about two metres in diameter, and glimmered faintly in the gloomy light.

"That's a nice ball of foil you have there, Freddy," said Jo, stepping out of the shadows. The others stood close behind her.

Freddy squinted at the Five from beneath an extremely dirty pair of eyebrows.

"Run away!" he croaked, beginning to push his foil ball ahead of him. "Run away!"

24

The Five glanced at each other as Freddy hobbled out of the alley with surprising speed. Then they gave chase.

Freddy limped along the street, glancing over his shoulder as the Five pelted round the corner after him. Swerving rapidly, he rolled his foil ball into a nearby laundrette. Undeterred, the Five followed. The laundrette door swung a couple of times, before Freddy emerged covered in soap suds, his foil ball a little cleaner than before. Moments later, the Five pushed through the door after him, trying to shake themselves free from a blanket of soap bubbles.

Puffing and panting, Freddy tried a beauty supply shop next, several doors down from the laundrette. Still spluttering bubbles, the Five chased him inside. Freddy burst into the street again, pushing a large Afro wig out of his eyes. Still in hot pursuit, the cousins emerged, also wearing an assortment of peculiar wigs.

"Keep running!" Freddy panted, racing into a paint shop on the other side of the street. His Afro wig was in danger of falling off. "Keep running away!"

Predictably, Freddy and the Five all emerged from the paint shop in a bright array of rainbow colours.

"I really prefer outdoor chases," Allie panted to no one in particular, holding on tight to her spiky punk wig and dripping an assortment of soap bubbles and paint colours on the pavement.

Freddy was picking up speed as the pavement sloped downhill. Or, more accurately, the foil ball was picking up speed.

"Run away! Run away!" Freddy shouted. His ball was starting to get ahead of him. "Catch up!" he added. "Catch up!"

He dived sideways to grab the ball, and promptly got steamrollered. Over and over tumbled the foil, glinting in the sunlight. Over and over went Freddy, looking increasingly dented as the Five sprinted down the hill after him.

CRASSSHHH!!

The ball reached the bottom of the slope and crunched into a group of dustbins. The bins went flying like skittles. Freddy tumbled through the air and landed neatly in the largest bin of all.

"Whew! It reeks of rubbish!" Freddy

moaned. "Wait," he said, sniffing himself intently. "That's me."

"Why did you poison our tree?" Jo demanded, pushing her corn-row wig out of her eyes and leaning on a nearby dustbin to catch her breath.

"I didn't!" Freddy spluttered. With the rubbish all over him, he looked more peculiar than ever. "Are you crazy?"

"No," Dylan said. "You are."

Allie pointed an accusing, paint-spattered finger at Freddy. "We know you bought— Dylan?"

"Metadexahydratin," Dylan obliged.

Freddy sniffed. "Yeah, I bought it," he said, picking a banana skin off his shoulder. "A bloke paid me to buy it for him. Secret-like. He was quite tall and chubby, bad skin. A mole on his neck that I'd have checked out if I was him."

"Gumptybum!" Jo gasped. "I knew there was something fishy about him. He must have poisoned the tree just so we'd pay him to do the repairs."

"That is *so* not nice," said Allie, shaking her head.

"If you didn't poison our tree," Max said, "how come you ran from us just now?"

"I thought you wanted my foil ball," Freddy whined. "No one can touch it – it's my retirement fund. I'm gonna charge people 50 pence to look at it." He glanced craftily at the Five. "Hup! You looked at it – you owe me two quid. Hup! You looked at it again! That's four quid."

"Wow," Dylan said, looking away in a hurry. "Now I don't know if I want to go into the rock business or the foil ball business."

Chapter Six

". . . Though the clean-up business is looking ever more lucrative," Dylan murmured.

Dylan, Max and Allie gaped at the mess that greeted them back at Jo's house. The study had been ransacked. Furniture lay on its side, and a bookshelf was hanging off the wall.

"Aunt George's study looks like a giant snow globe that somebody shook really hard," said Max, fumbling for a description as Timmy sniffed at the chaos. "And everything came loose, and then the snow melted." He paused. "And for some reason, there are cushions."

"There's no sign of my parents anywhere," said

Jo, coming into the study with a flustered expression on her face. "Nor Ed Gumptybum."

Timmy nosed underneath the desk and picked up a bag of crisps with his teeth.

"There *is* a sign of Ed Gumptybum," Dylan said, pointing at Timmy. "Those are the crisps he eats."

Jo bit her lip. "I hope my parents are all right," she said. "We'd better report this to Constable Stubblefield right away."

She left the room. So did Max and Dylan, both shaking their heads. Allie made to follow, but was caught in the full glare of Timmy's Big Eyes. Timmy wrinkled his eyebrows for extra oomph, the bag of crisps still in his mouth.

"Must . . . look . . . away . . ." Allie gasped, holding up her hands hopelessly. Then: "Can't!" She seized the crisps from Timmy's mouth and tore open the packet. "Oh, well," she said, tossing Timmy a handful of crisps. "I guess a few potato chips can't hurt . . ."

Down at the Falcongate police station, the kids hovered around Constable Stubblefield's vacant desk. A note was taped to her computer screen.

"Have gone to Romance Novel Book Fair for seminar on How To Tame The Rebel Heart Of A Pirate Captain Whose Mistress Is The Sea . . ." Jo read, leaning in close to the note. "Back at four p.m."

Max noticed a paperback romance lying on the desk and picked it up with a snort. "Can you believe people read these cheesy things?" he said. "Hmm, 'Colonel Hawthorne seized the proud Cornelia in his whip-strong arms, his coal-black eyes burning through her icy reserve.'" He stopped, an odd expression in his eyes. "Hmm," he said. "That's oddly compelling."

"How cute!" Allie gasped, groping around for her phone. "Max is turning into a teenage girl! I've got to get a picture . . ." She looked down at the phone screen. "Ooh, memory's full – I've got to delete some stuff . . ."

She started to hit some buttons.

"Look," said Jo, stopping Allie's hand. "You can see Ed Gumptybum's van in that picture." She squinted at Allie's tiny phone screen. "I can't make out the number plate . . ."

Dylan addressed Constable Stubblefield's empty

chair. "Constable Stubblefield?" he said loudly. "Is it OK if we use your computer? Just say 'no' if you don't want us to."

He cocked his head in a pretence of listening.

"Guess she doesn't mind," he concluded. Holding out his hand for Allie's phone, he plugged it into a cable connected to the computer.

The picture of George with leaves in her face appeared on the computer screen. Ed Gumptybum's van was clearly visible in the background. Dylan tapped some keys, cropped the image of the van and enlarged it until the number plate was visible.

"Constable Stubblefield," Dylan asked the screen. "Is it OK if we log on to your motor vehicle database so we can trace an owner? Just say 'no' if it's not."

He cocked his head to listen once more to the computer's gentle whirring. "Thanks," Dylan said cheerfully to the screen. "You're very helpful."

"'Cornelia yearned for Hawthorne with every beat of her heart,'" Max read aloud from the romance novel as Dylan tapped a few more keys. "'But she could only think of him as the man who killed her brother.'" He stared over the top of the

book at the others, aghast. "Hawthorne killed her brother?! Theirs is a doomed love!"

"This is weird," Dylan said, sitting back and studying the screen. "The van's not registered to Ed Gumptybum, it's registered to 'Edgar Stick'."

"Edgar Stick?!" Jo gasped. "I know that name. There's a whole entry in my mum's journal about him and his parents. They were horrible people!"

Allie frowned. "So, if we're saying that Ed Gumptybum is actually Edgar Stick, then . . . he probably didn't poison the tree just to rustle up some work for himself. But then, why did he?"

"Maybe the answer's back in my mum's study," Jo said.

They all turned at a loud choking noise. Timmy cocked a dubious eyebrow at Max.

"I had to skip to the last page," Max sniffled, wiping his eyes. "Hawthorne and Cornelia end up together!"

Chapter Seven

The cousins crawled around George's trashed study, gathering up the torn journal pages.

"Hmm," said Dylan, settling back on one of the scatter cushions with a handful of pages. "All of these pages are about the Sticks and Kirrin Island."

"These, too," said Max, waving another bunch of papers. "No offence to your mum, Jo, but this is pretty dry stuff compared to Colonel Hawthorne and Cornelia."

"Well," said Allie, not looking up from her section of the torn-up journal, "you didn't have the part about how the Sticks hid stolen treasure in the Kirrin Island dungeons."

Dylan brightened. "And if there's still loot there, there could be a big reward," he said. "Fame. The Queen could knight us." He paused, thinking. "Er, no," he said at last, "I'd rather have the money."

"Well," Allie said, "if Stick tore these up, they must have made him really mad."

"Or maybe he wanted them and my mum tore them up so he couldn't get them," Jo said thoughtfully.

Dylan wriggled to get more comfortable on his cushions. "But where is your mum?" he asked Jo. "And where's everyone else?"

Timmy was sitting beside Jo, looking up at the painting of Kirrin Island. He jumped up, put his paws against the wall and barked at the picture.

Jo went to the painting and studied it.

"This is my mum's boat key," she said, pulling the key on its yellow keychain out of the frame.

"She should just get one of those hooks by the door and hang them there," Max said, scratching his head. "'Cos it kind of ruins that painting."

Jo's face blazed with excitement as she faced the others. "The painting is of Kirrin Island," she said. "I bet my mum stuck this key here as a clue."

Dylan got to his feet. "Well, we've got a boat key," he said, pulling Allie and Max up. "We've got a boat. What are we waiting for?"

And as one, the Five stared at the picture of Kirrin Island, standing like a fortress in a swirling sea.

Kirrin Island stood some way offshore, not far from Shelter Island where Jo and her cousins had recently had a crazy adventure. Kirrin Island and its ruined castle had belonged to George's family for years. It was part of the Kirrin family legend that George and her cousins had once found gold in the castle dungeons – gold which had paid for George's education and set up the Kirrins for life. The castle stood in proud ruins on top of the island, promising further secrets and adventures for anyone bold enough to look for them.

Ed Gumptybum's daughter Gwen was driving a sleek little motorboat towards the island. Ed sat in the middle of the boat, keeping an eye on George and Ravi, who were both bound up in a selection of ropes and curtains from the study.

"You're wasting your time, Spotty Face," said

George mulishly, struggling with her bonds. "I'm not going to show you anything."

Ed wagged a pudgy finger at George. "Oh, you'd better," he advised. "Or you and your husband won't be coming back from that island."

Later that day, the Five climbed out of George's small wooden boat on the shore of Kirrin Island, after a tricky bit of steering round some craggy, fierce-looking rocks. They gazed towards a stretch of steep cliffs above them.

"Does the journal say where to find the secret tunnel in the cliffs?" Dylan asked hopefully.

"Well," Jo said, flicking through the pages, "there are three pages about an eggs-beans-and-bangers breakfast, with great detail about the butter, but only one sentence about the secret tunnel in the cliffs, and I quote, 'We found a secret tunnel in the cliffs.'"

The cousins gazed up at the wide expanse of rock. Where were they going to start looking for the mouth of a tunnel?

Timmy sniffed around. His tail started wagging, and he took off towards a crumbling section of the

cliff. Jo, Max, Allie and Dylan hurried after him.

"It's a trail," Dylan whooped, as Timmy nosed aside some bushes and revealed a stony path. "Could it lead to the secret entrance? Where else would it lead? Why am I asking all the questions?"

Chapter Eight

In the medieval dungeons beneath what was once Kirrin Castle, Ed locked George into a set of rusty iron shackles set in the stone wall. Nearby, Ravi was hanging upside down from some shackles set in the dungeon ceiling. His coat dangled down, covering the upper half of his body.

The dungeon was crowded with treasure: small marble statues, gold vases, silver candelabra, heaps of jewels and scattered piles of gold and silver coins. Gwen was busy loading the swag into a wheelbarrow as Ed adjusted George's shackles and stepped back to admire his work.

"You're exactly like your parents," George

shouted, wriggling furiously. "Locking people up in dungeons. Rude, rude, rude."

"But unlike his parents," Gwen said as she took up the handles of the groaning, glittering wheelbarrow, "he's going to get away with it. And if he knows what's good for him," she added, "he's going to buy me an open-top sports car."

"Feeling . . . light . . . headed," said Ravi in a woozy voice from somewhere underneath the folds of his coat.

"Shut your yap," Ed ordered.

"Shutting yap," said Ravi obediently.

Ed turned to his daughter. "Gwen, sweetie, wheel that stuff down to the dock so we can load up."

Stopping briefly to put a sparkly tiara on her head, Gwen pushed the wheelbarrow out of the door.

"And what do you plan to do with us?" George asked coldly.

Ed shrugged. "I thought I'd just leave you here forever."

"Then I'm going to need an aspirin," said Ravi in a muffled voice.

Out on the Kirrin cliffs, the cousins scrambled up the steep, rocky trail that Timmy had found. Rocks slid out from underneath them as they scrabbled higher and higher. The beach looked a long way down.

At the front, Jo nearly lost her footing as the trail simply stopped. The Five clung to the cliff and stared at each other.

"The trail ends here," Jo said. "No trace of a secret entrance."

Timmy's nose got to work again. Sniffing at the end of the trail, he plunged into another set of bushes, digging away at their shallow roots until he exposed a small hole in the cliff face.

"He's found the entrance!" Max said in relief. "Good going, Timmy!"

Jo relaxed. "Good boy, Timmy," she said happily, rubbing Timmy's coat as he gave her the Big-Eye treatment. Jo struggled briefly, before saying: "Well, I guess you've earned a treat. Just this once, you can have a biscuit."

Pulling a biscuit from the pocket of her fleece, she tossed it to Timmy.

"There are biscuits?" said Max indignantly as Timmy wolfed down his treat. "Why wasn't I informed?"

With a sigh, Jo tossed Max a biscuit as well.

Timmy finished his biscuit with a whine of contentment. Then he enthusiastically started through the small entrance he found. But his rather wide girth meant that within moments, he was stuck.

"He's too fat to go through!" Allie wailed, clutching on to Dylan and trying not to look down.

"It's my fault! I've been sneaking him treats!"

"Me, too," Dylan groaned.

"Me three," Max added sheepishly.

"I told you guys not to give him treats," Jo tutted. "Why'd you do it?"

"Why'd *you* give him a biscuit?" Allie countered.

Jo looked uncomfortable. " 'Cos . . . he looked at me," she said.

"So no more treats for Timmy," Max said. "But right now, we'd better give him the old heave-ho."

Scrabbling in the loose stones for some kind of grip, the cousins all pushed against Timmy's backside. It didn't budge. Timmy whined, his head wedged inside the cliff.

"The old heave-ho isn't working," said Dylan, stopping to wipe the sweat off his glasses. "Let's give him the new *improved* heave-ho."

With renewed effort, they pushed again. With a *pop*, Timmy squeezed through the entrance. Wriggling through after Timmy, the cousins found themselves in a long, dark, stone corridor. They turned on their torches and hurried along the passageway until they emerged into a small, empty

stone chamber. It looked like they had reached a dead end.

"We arrived in a bare, stone chamber which looked like a dead end," Jo murmured, angling her torch so that she could read the torn piece of journal in her hand. "Luckily, Julian discovered a hidden door."

The others didn't need telling twice. They stretched out their hands and started checking the walls for hidden latches. They swept the room three times, wiggling their fingers into every nook and crevice they could find. Nothing clicked, and nothing opened.

"I've been over every centimetre of this wall," Jo said, sitting back in defeat. "There's no door in it."

The others slumped against the wall beside Jo, exhausted from their efforts. To their surprise, their combined weight caused the entire wall to pivot, depositing them in another corridor.

Max blinked at the new view. "That was a fun one," he said.

Stretching directly in front of them, a long stone staircase twisted up and out of view. In excitement, Allie hurried up it, taking the steps two at a time.

"'The stone staircase leading out of the chamber had quite a little surprise'," Jo read from the diary, puffing a little as the others raced after Allie up the staircase. "'The top step . . .'"

Allie reached the top step of the stairs and plummeted out of sight.

"Aaaahhhh!!!" she squealed.

"'. . . was a trapdoor'," Jo finished, pausing at the top of the stair and gazing down at Allie, who was now clinging to the top step and dangling over a deep shaft with terror in her eyes.

Chapter Nine

Down below, Ed and Gwen were wheeling the last barrowful of loot out of the dungeon. Gwen had added a sparkling diamond necklace round her neck to match her tiara, and her fingers were weighted with rings.

"Well," said Ed, turning and saluting George and Ravi at the door, "it's been grand, but it's time for us to go. Hope you guys have a nice time 'hanging out'!" He laughed evilly at his own joke.

"Could you throw me a magazine on your way out?" Ravi asked.

The dungeon door clanged shut. George and Ravi were left in the dark. After a moment of

silence, George said:

"Ravi? Let's sing."

"Sorry, dear," Ravi said, "maybe it's just the blood rushing to my head, but I thought you suggested singing."

George wriggled against her shackles. "We have to do something to keep our spirits up," she said. "And we can hardly play cricket just now can we?"

"That's my little chickpea," said Ravi fondly, swinging slightly from his ankles. "Always trying to look on the bright side." He held his hands up to his head. "Ooh," he added weakly. "Seeing. Stars."

Over the deep shaft at the top of the secret staircase, there wasn't a moment to lose. Jo grabbed Allie's hand. It slipped from her grasp. Max dived forward with Jo, grabbing at Allie's wrist, while Dylan clung on to Max's ankles so he didn't get dragged down. Keen to help, Timmy sank his teeth into the seat of Dylan's jeans and heaved.

"Careful there, Timmy," Dylan panted, pulling hard at Max's ankles. "That's not rump steak."

With one almighty heave, the cousins collapsed

back on the staircase as Allie struggled to safety.

"There's no way this castle meets current building safety standards," said Allie furiously, brushing at the dirt and cobwebs on her clothes as she got to her feet.

They climbed carefully over the gaping hole to stand in the corridor which opened up ahead. Muffled voices drifted towards them.

"In South Australia I was born . . ." sang George in an echoey kind of way.

"Heave heave – all the way home!" Ravi boomed.

"It's my parents!" Jo said. "They sing sea shanties when they're in trouble!"

"In South Australia round Cape Horn . . ." George continued.

"Heave, heave all the way home!" Ravi roared.

Jo raced down the corridor with the others close behind her. Rusty old suits of armour lined the walls, looking eerily like a ghost army. Ducking and weaving through clanking bits of armour, Jo pushed an outstretched iron arm out of her way. There was the flip of a secret switch.

Click.

Before the Five had time to stop running, the

corridor floor ahead of them fell away, forming a long chute that disappeared into the gloom. Helplessly they skidded on to the chute and slid downwards at full speed.

"Heave, heave," George and Ravi sang, winding up their song. "All the way—"

"AAAAahhhh!"

Jo, Allie, Dylan and Max shot through a hole in the dungeon roof and hit the floor in a heap.

"—home!" George and Ravi finished, grinning at the children in delight.

Max struggled to his feet. "We have got to do that again!" he said, his face ablaze with excitement.

WHOOSH!

Timmy was the last out of the chute, landing on top of Max in a blur of black, white and brown fur.

"Ooof!" said Max, crashing backwards. "That's a ton of Timmy."

"Mum! Dad!" Jo said, getting up and rushing across the dungeon floor to her parents. "Are you OK?"

"We're fine," George said. "But Ed and Gwen are getting away with a fortune!"

"A fortune?!" cried Dylan in an eager voice,

quickly getting up. "Sir Dylan to the rescue! Reward time!"

The Five dashed out of the dungeon, leaving George and Ravi behind.

"Don't worry about us!" said Ravi after a moment. He was sounding very light-headed. "Blood . . . rushing . . . to . . .head . . . Oohh, it's actually quite pleasant now. Hmmmmm!"

Chapter Ten

The Sticks had loaded their motorboat with loot and were now ploughing through the choppy sea, weaving through the rocks with reckless abandon and heading for the opening in the reef which fringed Kirrin Island. Gwen was at the tiller, while Ed was busy rearranging treasure at the bottom of the boat.

"Dad," said Gwen. "We've got a problem."

"I know," Ed tutted happily. "What do we buy first? A house on the French Riviera or our own Mediterranean island? Both. Ha ha. Problem solved."

"No," Gwen said. "Look!"

Ed looked up to see the Five in their boat, approaching the reef opening from the ocean side.

"We're beating them to the reef!" Allie screamed.

"Perfect," said Jo, studying the journal in between heaving on the tiller.

"But they're turning," Max noticed. "They're getting away!"

Indeed, Gwen had slowed the boat and was turning back, heading towards another gap in the reef.

"Even more perfect," Jo said, heaving on the tiller. "The journal says there's a wrecked ship just below the water line, 'twenty-eight yards due west of the reef'. And we're driving them right towards it!"

Dylan punched the air in triumph. "Finally," he said, "the journal gets specific!"

Down in the dark blue water around the edges of the reef, the hulk of an old wooden ship could be seen. About two metres of its jagged, broken mast stuck up above the waves. The Five pursued the Sticks, driving them unwittingly towards their downfall.

"See yer around, kids!" Ed chortled, failing to

notice the broken mast as they ploughed towards it. "Don't let any trees fall on yer! Ha, ha, ha!"

There was a grinding, crunching sound deep in the hull of the motorboat.

"Ohh," said Ed uneasily, peering around. "What was that? We're slowing down."

Caught on the old mast, their boat slowed right down to a crawl.

"Ahoy, maties," said Jo cheerfully, pulling up alongside the Sticks. "What happened – a tree fall on your boat?"

"No," Ed snarled, "just a little leak. We'll get it patched and send you a postcard from the Riviera!"

Timmy launched himself from George's boat and landed with a thump in the Sticks' boat. The small hole formed by the wreck's mast suddenly turned into an enormous one as Timmy plunged right through the weakened wood and into the water below. The motorboat immediately started sinking, taking its statues and jewels with it. Coughing and spluttering, Ed and Gwen swam towards the mast of the wreck and clung on.

"The police are on their way," Dylan yelled gleefully. "Send us a postcard from prison."

Allie pulled a bottle from her purse and tossed it to the Sticks. "It'll be a while till they get here," she advised. "Here's some sunscreen. SPF 30!"

As Ed and Gwen fought over the little bottle of sunscreen, Timmy paddled towards George's boat and tried to climb in. The cousins heaved and hauled at him, struggling to get him out of the water.

"So," Jo gasped, straining with the effort, "we're all agreed—"

"No . . . more . . . treats . . . for Timmy!" groaned the others, pulling with all their might and hauling the tubby hound on board.

Allie reached into the water and grabbed a bejewelled necklace which was about to join its friends at the bottom of the sea. She fixed it round Timmy's neck.

"At least," she said fondly, sitting back to admire the effect, "no food treats. Oooh. Stylin' . . ."

A little later, the Five were back in the dungeon with Jo's parents. Jo unshackled George. Ravi was still hanging upside down.

"I never care to see this dungeon again," George said, rubbing at her wrists where the shackles had been chafing. "Right, Ravi?"

Ravi's only answer was an hysterical giggle.

"You'd better get your Uncle Ravi down, kids," George advised. "He's getting giddy."

"Please," giggled Ravi, "just five more minutes. He he he he!"

A week later, with no villains to chase, treasure to find, or parents to rescue, the cousins had fixed up

a small skateboarding ramp at the side of Jo's house and were taking turns doing tricks off it.

A slimmer Timmy ran happily alongside Jo as she angled her board and raced for the ramp, doing a high jump off the top. Timmy jumped after her. Swinging back round, Jo did the same thing again – only this time, she went higher. Undeterred, Timmy did the same, flying high over George's prize cactus garden in Jo's slipstream.

Dylan was next. He narrowed his eyes, lined up his skateboard and took a run at the ramp. He jumped, doubled back and jumped again, aiming to clear the cactus garden the same way that Jo and Timmy had. Unfortunately, he hadn't picked up as much speed as his cousin and her dog. With a *whump* and a groan of pain, he landed smack on a cactus.

"Timmy's back in shape now," Dylan panted, rubbing his bottom. "But I guess I'm a bit flabby." He attempted Timmy's Big-Eyes look. "Don't give me any treats, anybody, whatever you do."

Opening his mouth, he waited for someone to toss him a treat. Allie, Max and Jo looked at him, turned their skateboards and headed in the opposite

direction. Timmy woofed sympathetically.

"It was worth a try," Dylan sighed, getting to his feet and scrambling back on to his board.

Epilogue

The next day, the Five were out in their boat, sailing close to the shore. Max was in charge of Dylan's camera.

"Sticky Situation Number Forty-Six: Falling Overboard," Max declared, fiddling with the lens and settling the camera against his eye.

Jo positioned herself so that Max could see both her and Dylan.

"Falling overboard can be quite dangerous," Jo said. She glanced enquiringly at Dylan for a demonstration. "Dylan . . . ?"

"But, the water's cold," Dylan protested.

"Dylan . . ." Allie wheedled.

With a sigh, Dylan jumped into the sea with an ungainly splash.

Allie moved into shot as Dylan flailed around in the water behind her. "You should always wear a life-jacket," she said, taking over from Jo. "But if you don't have one you can improvise by removing your pants."

Treading water, Dylan took off his trousers.

"Tie knots at the ends of the legs," Jo continued, "then throw the open end – the waist – down into the water."

"This traps air in the pants," Allie said as Dylan did as Jo had instructed. "Put your head between the inflated legs, and use it as an emergency life jacket."

Dylan obediently tucked his head between the legs of the inflated trousers, and held on to the ends. Allie and Jo leaned over and pulled him aboard.

"But if you're wearing teddy-bear patterned underwear," Jo smirked as Dylan crawled aboard, "it can be embarrassing when you're rescued."

"Put me back in the water!" Dylan howled, trying to cover his teddy-decorated boxers as Max

zoomed in for the finishing shot with a shout of laughter.